DAVID McPHAIL

I Had Ten Hats

I Like to Read®

HOLIDAY HOUSE • NEW YORK

I had a rain hat.

I had a sun hat.

I had a snow hat.

I had a bike hat.

I had a bat hat.

I had a hard hat.

I had a flat hat.

I had a cat hat.

I had a red hat.

I had a bed hat.

I had ten hats.

Can you help me find them?

Thank you.

For Luke and David Peter

I LIKE TO READ is a registered trademark of Holiday House Publishing, Inc.

Copyright © 2021 by David McPhail
All Rights Reserved
HOLIDAY HOUSE is registered in the U.S. Patent and Trademark Office.
Printed and bound in March 2021 at C&C Offset, Shenzhen, China.
The artwork was made with watercolor over pen and ink.
www.holidayhouse.com
First Edition
1 3 5 7 9 10 8 6 4 2

This book has been officially leveled by using the F&P Text Level Gradient™ Leveling System.

Library of Congress Cataloging-in-Publication Data

Names: McPhail, David, 1940– author, illustrator.
Title: I had ten hats / David McPhail.
Description: New York : Holiday House, [2021] | Series: I like to read
Audience: Ages 4–8. | Audience: Grades K–1. | Summary: "Have fun finding
silly hats—a flat hat, a bat hat, and even a cat hat"— Provided by publisher.
Identifiers: LCCN 2020035851 | ISBN 9780823448593 (hardcover)
Subjects: CYAC: Hats—Fiction.
Classification: LCC PZ7.M478818 Iae 2021 | DDC [E]—dc23
LC record available at https://lccn.loc.gov/2020035851

ISBN 9780823448593 (hardcover)